Judy
Moody

The author extends special thanks
to Hailey and Randi Reel.

ISBN 0-439-16626-8

12 11 10 9 8 7 6 5 4 3   1 2 3 4 5/0

Printed in the U.S.A.   40

First Scholastic printing, October 2000

This book was typeset in Stone Informal.
The illustrations were done in watercolor, tea, and pen and ink.

Judy Moody

Megan McDonald

illustrated by
Peter Reynolds

SCHOLASTIC INC.

New York Toronto London Auckland Sydney
Mexico City New Delhi Hong Kong

For my sisters, Susan, Deborah, Michele, Melissa
M. M.

For my daughter, Sarah, and her cat, Twinkles
P. R.

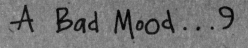
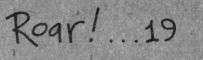

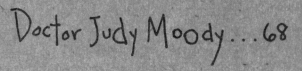

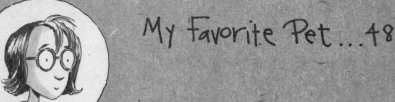

Mouse

Rocky

Frank

Mr. Todd

A Bad Mood

Judy Moody did not want to give up summer. She did not feel like brushing her hair every day. She did not feel like memorizing spelling words. And she did not want to sit next to Frank Pearl, who ate paste, in class.

Judy Moody was in a mood.

Not a good mood. A bad mood. A mad-face mood. Even the smell of her new Grouchy pencils could not get her out of bed.

"First day of school!" sang her mother. "Shake a leg and get dressed."

Judy Moody slunk down under the covers and put a pillow over her head.

"Judy? Did you hear me?"

"ROAR!" said Judy.

She would have to get used to a new desk and a new classroom. Her new desk would not have an armadillo sticker with her name on it, like her old one last year. Her new classroom would not have a porcupine named Roger.

And with her luck, she'd get stuck sitting in the first row, where Mr. Todd could see every time she tried to pass a note to her best friend, Rocky.

Mom poked her head inside Judy's room

again. "And think about brushing that hair, okay?"

One of the worst things about the first day of school was that everybody came back from summer wearing new T-shirts that said DISNEY WORLD or SEA WORLD or JAMESTOWN: Home of Pocahontas. Judy searched her top drawer and her bottom drawer and even her underwear drawer. She could not find one shirt with words.

She wore her tiger-striped pajama pants on the bottom and a plain old no-words T-shirt on top.

"She's wearing pajamas!" said her brother, Stink, when she came downstairs. "You can't wear pajamas to school!"

Stink thought he knew everything now that he was starting second grade. Judy glared at him with one of her famous troll-eyes stares.

"Judy can change after breakfast," Mom said.

"I made sunny-side-up eggs for the first day of school," said Dad. "There's squishy bread for dipping."

There was nothing sunny about Judy's egg—the yellow middle was broken. Judy slid her wobbly egg into the napkin on her lap, and fed it to Mouse, their cat, under the table.

"Summer is over, and I didn't even go anywhere," said Judy.

"You went to Gramma Lou's," said Mom.

"But that was right here in boring old Virginia. And I didn't get to eat hot dogs and ride a roller coaster or see a whale," said Judy.

"You rode a bumper car," said Mom.

"Baby cars. At the mall," Judy said.

"You went fishing and ate shark," said Dad.

"She ate a shark?" asked Stink.

"I ate a shark?" asked Judy.

"Yes," said Dad. "Remember the fish we bought at the market when we couldn't catch any?"

"I ate a shark!" said Judy Moody.

Judy Moody ran back to her room and peeled off her shirt. She took out a fat marker and drew a big-mouthed shark with lots of teeth. I ATE A SHARK, she wrote in all capitals.

Judy ran out the door to the bus. She didn't wait for Stink. She didn't wait for kisses from Dad or hugs from Mom. She was in a hurry to show Rocky her new T-shirt with words.

She almost forgot her bad mood until she saw Rocky practicing card tricks at the bus stop. He was wearing a giant-sized blue and white T-shirt with fancy letters and a picture of the Loch Ness Monster roller coaster.

"Like my new T-shirt?" he asked. "I got it at Busch Gardens."

"No," said Judy Moody, even though she secretly liked the shirt.

"I like your shark," said Rocky. When Judy didn't say anything, he asked, "Are you in a bad mood or something?"

"Or something," said Judy Moody.

Roar!

When Judy Moody arrived in third grade, her teacher, Mr. Todd, stood by the door, welcoming everyone. "Hello there, Judy."

"Hello, Mr. Toad," said Judy. She cracked herself up.

"Class, please hang your backpacks on the hooks and put your lunches in the cubbies," said Mr. Todd.

Judy Moody looked around the classroom.

"Do you have a porcupine named Roger?" Judy asked Mr. Todd.

"No, but we have a turtle named Tucson. Do you like turtles?"

She liked turtles! But she caught herself just in time. "No. I like toads." Judy cracked up again.

"Rocky, your seat is over by the window, and Judy, yours is right up front," said Mr. Todd.

"I knew it," said Judy. She surveyed her new front-row desk. It didn't have an armadillo sticker with her name on it.

Guess Who sat across the aisle from her. Frank Eats-Paste Pearl. He glanced at Judy sideways, then bent his thumb all the way back, touching his wrist. Judy

rolled her tongue like a hot dog back at him.

"You like sharks too?" he asked, passing her a small white envelope with her name on it.

Ever since they had danced the Maypole together in kindergarten, this boy would not leave her alone. In first grade, Frank Pearl sent her five valentines. In second grade, he gave her a cupcake on Halloween, on Thanksgiving, and on Martin Luther King, Jr. Day. Now, on the first day of third grade, he gave her a birthday party invitation. Judy checked the date inside—his birthday was not for three weeks! Even a real shark would not scare him off.

"Can I look inside your desk?" asked Judy. He moved to one side. No sign of paste.

Mr. Todd stood in front of the class. GINO'S EXTRA-CHEESE PIZZA was printed in large letters on the board.

"Are we having extra-cheese pizza for lunch?" Judy asked.

"For Spelling." Mr. Todd held his finger to his lips like it was a secret. "You'll see."

Then he said, "Okay! Third grade! Listen up! We're going to try something different to kick off the year, as a way of getting to know one another. This year, each of you will make your own Me collage. All about YOU. You can draw or cut out pictures and paste things to your collage that tell the class what makes you YOU."

A Me collage! It sounded fun to Judy, but she didn't say so.

"We don't have to draw a map of our family, then?" asked Jessica Finch.

"I'm passing out a list of ideas for things you might include, like your family. I'm also giving everyone a folder for collecting the things you want to put on your collage. We'll work on these as we have time over the next month. At the end of September, you'll each get a chance to tell the class about YOU."

All through Language Arts and Social Studies, Judy thought about one thing— herself. Judy Moody, star of her own Me collage. Maybe third grade wasn't so bad after all.

"Okay, everybody. Time for Spelling."

"Yuck. Spelling," Judy said under her breath, remembering her bad mood.

"Yuck. Spelling," Frank Pearl agreed. Judy squinched her eyebrows at him.

"Take out a piece of paper and write down five spelling words you can find hidden in the words on the board, GINO'S EXTRA-CHEESE PIZZA."

"Cool Spelling, huh?" said a note passed to Judy by Frank.

"No," she wrote back on her hand, flashing it at him.

Judy took out her brand-new package of Grouchy pencils with mad faces on them. *GROUCHY pencils—for completely impossible moods,* said the package. *Ever see a pencil that looks like it got up on the wrong side of the bed?*

Perfect. The new Grouchy pencil helped her think. She found the words TREE, TEXAS, and TAXI hidden in Mr. Todd's spelling on the board. But instead she wrote down 1)NO 2)NO 3)NO 4)NO 5)NO.

"Who would like to tell the class five words they came up with?" asked Mr. Todd.

Judy's hand shot up.

"Judy?"

"NO, NO, NO, NO, NO!" said Judy.

"That's one word. I need four more. Come up and write them on the board."

Judy Moody did not write TREE,

TEXAS, and TAXI. Instead she wrote RAT and GNAT.

"How about BRAT?" called Rocky.

"There's no *B*," said Frank Pearl.

TIGER, wrote Judy.

"One more word," said Mr. Todd.

SPIT, wrote Judy.

"Can you use any of those words in a sentence, Judy?" asked Mr. Todd.

"The tiger spit on the rat and the gnat."

The whole class cracked up. Frank laughed so hard he snorted.

"Are you in a bad mood today?" asked Mr. Todd.

"ROAR," said Judy Moody.

"That's too bad," said Mr. Todd. "I was just about to ask who wants to go down to the office and pick up the pizza. It's a welcome-back surprise."

"Pizza? Pizza! For real?" The room buzzed with excitement.

Judy Moody wanted to be the one to pick up the pizza. She wanted to be the one to open the box. She wanted to be the one who got to keep the little three-legged plastic table that kept the box top from sticking to the pizza.

"So. Who would like to pick up the pizza today?" asked Mr. Todd.

"Me!" yelled Judy. "Me! Me! Me! Me! Me!" everyone shouted at once, waving their hands like windmills in the air.

Rocky raised his hand without saying a word.

"Rocky, would you like to pick up the pizza?"

"Sure!" said Rocky.

"Luck-y!" Judy said.

When Rocky came back with the pizza, the class grew quiet, everyone chewing teeny-weeny cheesy squares of Gino's pizza and listening to Mr. Todd read them a chapter from a book about a pepperoni pizza–eating dog.

When he finished reading, Judy asked, "Mr. Todd, can I look at your little pizza table?"

"That does look like a miniature table, Judy. I never thought of it that way."

"I collect them," said Judy Moody. She didn't really collect them—yet. So far, she had collections of twenty-seven dead moths, a handful of old scabs, a dozen fancy toothpicks, hundreds of designer Band-Aids (she needed the box tops), a box of body parts (from dolls!) including three Barbie heads, and four unused erasers shaped like baseballs.

"Tell you what," said Mr. Todd. "If you think you can come to third grade in a good mood tomorrow, it's yours. Do you think you can agree to that?"

"Yes, Mr. Todd," said Judy. "Yes, yes, yes, yes, YES!"

pizza table ↱

Two Heads are Better Than One

Judy was teaching Mouse to walk on two legs when the phone rang.

"Hello?"

All she heard was air.

"Hello?" Judy asked the air.

"Hello, Judy? Are you allowed to come to my party?" a voice asked. A Frank Pearl voice. It had only been two days since he gave her the invitation.

"Wrong number," said Judy, hanging up. She dangled her new pizza table from a string in front of Mouse's nose.

The phone rang again. "Hello? Is this the Moodys'?"

"Not now, Frank. I'm in the middle of an important experiment."

"Okay. Bye."

The phone rang a third time.

"The experiment's not over yet," Judy yelled into the phone.

"What experiment?" asked Rocky.

"Never mind," said Judy.

"Let's go to Vic's," said Rocky. "I want to get something for my Me collage." Vic's was the Mini Mart down the hill where they had cool prizes in the jawbreaker machine, like tattoos that wash off and magic tricks.

"Let me ask," said Judy.

"Mom, can I go to Vic's with Rocky?"

"Sure," said Mom.

"Sure!" said Judy, tossing Mouse the pizza table.

"I'm going too," said Stink.

"No, you're not," Judy told him.

"You and Rocky can take him along," said Mom, giving her one of those looks.

"But he doesn't know about crossing through China and Japan on the way," Judy said. Only best friends knew that the first speed bump on the way was crossing into China, the second, Japan.

"I'm sure you could teach him," Mom said.

"Teach me," said Stink.

"Meet me at the manhole," Judy said back into the phone. The manhole was exactly halfway between Judy's front door and Rocky's. Over the summer they had measured it with a very long ball of string.

She ran out the door. Stink ran out the door after her.

Rocky had a dollar. Judy had a dollar. Stink had six pennies.

"If we put our money together, we can buy eight jawbreakers," said Rocky.

"Two heads are better than one," Judy laughed. "Get it?" She unscrunched the dollar bill from her pocket and pointed to George Washington's head.

"I've got six heads," said Stink, showing his pennies.

"That's because you're a monster! Get it?" Judy and Rocky cracked up.

Rocky's

Judy's

stink's

Stink did not have enough money for even one jawbreaker. "You'll break your mouth if you try to eat eight jawbreakers," said Stink. "I could eat at least two for you."

"It's for the prizes," Judy told him.

"Eight quarters give us eight chances to win a magic trick," said Rocky. "I need a new magic trick to paste on my Me collage."

"Hey, wait!" said Judy. "I just remembered—I need my dollar to buy Band-Aids."

"Band-Aids are boring," said Stink. "Besides, you have ten million. Dad says we have more Band-Aids in our bathroom than the Red Cross."

"But I want to be a doctor," said Judy. "Like Elizabeth Blackwell, First Woman Doctor! She started her own hospital. She knew how to operate and put together body parts and everything."

"Body parts. Yuck!" Stink said.

"You saved Band-Aid box tops all summer," said Rocky. "I thought you had enough to send away for that doctor doll."

"I did. I already ordered it. Back in July. I'm still waiting for it to come. But now I need a microscope. You can look at blood or scabs or anything with it!"

Stink asked, "When do we get to China?"

"We're still on Jefferson Street, Stink," Rocky told him.

"Let's look for rocks until we get to China," said Stink.

"Let's see who can find the best one," said Rocky.

The three of them studied the ground as they walked. Judy found five pink pebbles and a Bazooka Joe comic with a fortune

5 pink pebbles bubblegum fortune

blue Lego

Lucky stone

that read: MONEY IS COMING YOUR WAY.
Rocky found a blue Lego and a stone with a
hole in the middle—a lucky stone!

"I found a black diamond!" said Stink.

"That's just charcoal," said Judy.

"It's just glass," Rocky said.

"Wait!" Judy said, crossing her eyes at
Rocky. "I think it's a moon rock! Don't you,
Rocky?"

"Yes," said Rocky. "Definitely."

"How do you know?" asked Stink.

"It has craters," Judy said.

"How did it get here?" asked Stink.

"It fell from the sky," said Judy.

"Really?" asked Stink.

"Really," said Rocky.

"In my *Space Junk* magazine, it tells how a moon rock fell from space and left a hole in Arizona once."

"And our teacher last year told us how a moon rock hit a dog in Egypt one time. No lie," Judy told her brother. "You're lucky. Moon rocks are billions of years old."

"*Space Junk* says moon rocks are dusty on the outside and sparkly on the inside," said Rocky.

"There's only one way to find out for sure if this is a moon rock then," said Judy. Judy scouted around for a large rock. Then she clobbered Stink's lump, smashing the moon rock to bits.

"You smashed it!" said Stink.

"Look, I think I see a sparkle!" said Rocky.

"Stink, you found a real moon rock, all right," Judy said.

"It's not a moon rock anymore!" cried Stink.

"Look at it this way, Stink," said Judy. "Now you have something better than a moon rock."

"What could be better than a moon rock?" asked Stink.

"Lots and lots of moon dust." Judy and Rocky fell down laughing.

"I'm going home," said Stink. He scraped up handfuls of the smashed rock, filling his pockets with dirt.

Judy and Rocky laughed the rest of the way to China, ran backward to Japan, then hopped on one foot while patting their heads until they got to Vic's.

At Vic's, they put their George Washington heads together for one small box of Band-Aids, and had enough left over for one jawbreaker each. Neither of them won a magic trick for Rocky's Me collage. Not even a troll or a miniature comic book or a tattoo.

"Maybe I could put a jawbreaker on my

collage," said Rocky. "Are you going to stick some Band-Aids on yours?"

"Hey, good idea," said Judy.

"Still a nickel left," Rocky said. So they bought a gumball and saved it for Stink.

When they reached Judy's driveway, Stink ran toward them, his pockets jangling with money. Stink had brown lunch bags lined up on the front steps.

"Guess what!" called Stink. "I made three dollars! Just since I got home."

"No way," said Judy.

"Let's see," said Rocky.

Stink emptied his pockets. Rocky counted twelve quarters.

"What's in the bags?" asked Judy.

"Everybody in the state of Virginia must want it."

"Yeah, what are you selling, anyway?" asked Rocky.

"Moon dust," said Stink.

50¢ A BAG

My Favorite Pet

It was Labor Day, a no-school day. Judy looked up from her Me collage on the dining-room table.

"We need a new pet," Judy announced to her family.

"A new pet? What's wrong with Mouse?" asked Mom. Mouse opened one eye.

"I have to pick MY FAVORITE PET. How can I pick my favorite when I only have one?"

"Pick Mouse," said Mom.

"Mouse is so old, and she's afraid of everything. Mouse is a lump that purrs."

"You're NOT thinking of a dog, I hope," said Dad. Mouse jumped off the chair and stretched.

"Mouse would definitely not like that," said Judy.

"How about a goldfish?" asked Stink. Mouse rubbed up against Judy's leg.

"Mouse would like that too much," Judy said. "I was thinking of a two-toed sloth."

"Right," said Stink.

"They're neat," said Judy. She showed Stink its picture in her rain forest magazine. "See? They hang upside down all day.

They even sleep upside down."

"You're upside down," said Stink.

"What do they eat?" asked Dad.

"It says here they eat leaf-cutter ants and fire-bellied toads," Judy read.

"That should be easy," said Stink.

"Tell you what, Judy," said Dad. "Let's take a ride over to the pet store. I'm not saying we'll get a sloth, but it's always fun to look around. Maybe it'll even help me think of a five-letter word for fish that starts with *M* for my crossword puzzle."

"Let's all go," said Mom.

When they arrived at Fur & Fangs, Judy saw snakes and parrots, hermit crabs and guppies. She even saw a five-letter fish word beginning with *M*—a black molly.

"Do you have any two-toed sloths?" she asked the pet store lady.

"Sorry. Fresh out," said the lady.

"How about a newt or a turtle?" asked Dad.

"Did you see the hamsters?" asked Mom.

"Never mind," said Judy. "There's nothing from the rain forest here."

"Maybe they have a stinkbug," Stink said.

"One's enough," said Judy, narrowing her eyes at Stink.

They picked out a squeaky toy mouse for Mouse. When they went to pay for it, Judy noticed a green plant with teeth sitting on the counter. "What's that?" she asked the pet store lady.

"A Venus flytrap," the lady said. "It's not

an animal, but it doesn't cost much, and it's easy to take care of. See these things that look like mouths with teeth? Each one closes like a trap door. It eats bugs around the house. Like flies and ants, that sort of thing. You can feed it a little raw hamburger too."

"Rare," said Judy Moody.

"Cool," said Stink.

"Good idea," said Mom.

"Sold," said Dad.

❦   ❦   ❦

Judy set her new pet on her desk, where the angle of sunlight hit it just right. Mouse watched from the bottom bunk, with one eye open.

"I can't wait to take my new pet to school

tomorrow for Share and Tell," Judy told
Stink. "It's just like a rare plant from the
rain forest."

"It is?" Stink asked.

"Sure," said Judy. "Just think. There
could be a medicine hiding right here in
these funny green teeth. When I'm a doctor,

I'm going to study plants like this and discover cures for ucky diseases."

"What are you going to name it?" asked Stink.

"I don't know yet," said Judy.

"You could call it Bughead, since it likes bugs."

"Nah," said Judy.

Judy watered her new pet. She sprinkled Gro-Fast on the soil. When Stink left, she sang songs to it. "I know an old lady who swallowed a fly. . . ." She sang till the old lady swallowed a horse.

She still couldn't think of a good name. Rumpelstiltskin? Too long. Thing? Maybe.

"Stink!" she called. "Go get me a fly."

"How am I going to catch a fly?" asked Stink.

"One fly. I'll give you a dime." Stink ran down to the window behind the couch and brought back a fly.

"Gross! That fly is dead."

"It was going to be dead in a minute anyway."

Judy scooped up the dead fly with the tip of her ruler and dropped it into one of the mouths. In a flash, the trap closed around the fly. Just like the pet store lady said.

"Rare!" said Judy.

"Snap! Trap!" Stink said, adding sound effects.

"Go get me an ant. A live one this time."

Here's one...

... a real beauty!

Here anty, anty!

No way!

Snap! Trap!

Urp!

Stink wanted to see the Venus flytrap eat again, so he got his sister an ant. "Snap! Trap!" said Judy and Stink when another trap closed.

"Double rare," Judy said.

"Stink, go catch me a spider or some-thing."

"I'm tired of catching bugs," said Stink.

"Then go ask Mom or Dad if we have any raw hamburger."

Stink frowned.

"Please, pretty please with bubble-gum ice cream on top?" Judy begged. Stink didn't budge. "I'll let you feed it this time."

Stink ran to the kitchen and came back with a hunk of raw hamburger. He plopped a big glob of hamburger into an open trap.

"That's way too much!" Judy yelled, but it was too late. The mouth snap-trapped around it, hamburger oozing out of its teeth. In a blink, the whole arm drooped, collapsing in the dirt.

"You killed it! You're in trouble, Stink. MOM! DAD!" Judy called.

Judy showed her parents what happened. "Stink killed my Venus flytrap!"

"I didn't mean to," said Stink. "The trap closed really fast!"

"It's not dead. It's digesting," said Dad. "The jaws will probably open by tomorrow morning," said Mom.

"Maybe it's just sleeping or something," said Stink.

"Or something," said Judy.

My Smelly Pet

Tomorrow morning came. The jaws were still closed. Judy tried teasing it with a brand new ant. "Here you go," she said in her best squeaky baby voice. "You like ants, don't you?" The jaws did not open one tiny centimeter. The plant did not move one trigger hair.

Judy gave up. She carefully lodged the plant in the bottom of her backpack. She'd take it to school, stinky, smelly glob of hamburger and all.

On the bus, Judy showed Rocky her new pet. "I couldn't wait to show everybody how it eats. Now it won't even move. And it smells."

"Open Sesame!" said Rocky, trying some magic words. Nothing happened.

"Maybe," said Rocky, "the bus will bounce it open."

"Maybe," said Judy. But even the bouncing of the bus did not make her new pet open up.

"If this thing dies, I'm stuck with Mouse for MY FAVORITE PET," Judy said.

Mr. Todd said first thing, "Okay, class, take out your Me collage folders. I'll pass around old magazines, and you can spend the next half-hour cutting out pictures for your collages. You still have over three weeks, but I'd like to see how everybody's doing."

Her Me collage folder! Judy had been so busy with her new pet, she had forgotten to bring her folder to school.

Judy Moody sneaked a peek at Frank Pearl's folder. He had cut out pictures of macaroni (favorite food?), ants (favorite pet?), and shoes. Shoes? Frank Pearl's best friend was a pair of shoes?

Judy looked down at the open backpack under her desk. The jaws were still closed. Now her whole backpack was smelly. Judy took the straw from her juice box and poked at the Venus flytrap. No luck. It would never open in time for Share and Tell!

"Well?" Frank asked.

"Well, what?"

"Are you going to come?"

"Where?"

"My birthday party. A week from Saturday. All the boys from our class are coming. And Adrian and Sandy from next door."

Judy Moody did not care if the president himself was coming. She sniffed her backpack. It stunk like a skunk!

"What's in your backpack?" Frank asked.

"None of your beeswax," Judy said.

"It smells like dead tuna fish!" Frank

Pearl said. Judy hoped her Venus flytrap would come back to life and bite Frank Pearl before he ever had another birthday.

Mr. Todd came over. "Judy, you haven't cut out any pictures. Do you have your folder?"

"I did—I mean—it was—then—well—no," said Judy. "I got a new pet last night."

"Don't tell me," said Mr. Todd. "Your new pet ate your Me collage folder."

"Not exactly. But it did eat one dead fly and one live ant. And then a big glob of . . ."

"Next time try to remember to bring your folder to school, Judy. And please, everyone, keep homework away from animals!"

"My new pet's not an animal, Mr. Todd," Judy said. "And it doesn't eat homework. Just bugs and raw hamburger." She pulled the Venus flytrap from her backpack. Judy could not believe her eyes! Its arm was no longer droopy. The stuck trap was now wide open, and her plant was looking hungry.

"It's MY FAVORITE PET," said Judy. "Meet Jaws!"

Doctor Judy Moody

Finally! Judy thought the only thing finer in the world than getting Jaws had to be getting a big brown box in the mail with the name DOCTOR Judy Moody on it. She was in an operating mood.

"Can I open it?" asked Stink, coming out of his closet fort.

"What does it say right there?" asked Judy, pointing to the label.

"Doctor Judy Moody," read Stink.

"Exactly," said Judy Moody. "I collected all the box tops."

"I got you some from the school nurse!" said Stink.

"Okay. You can go get the scissors."

Stink handed over the scissors. Judy poked through the tape and broke open the brown flaps. Mouse pawed at the sticky tape. Stink's head kept getting in the way.

"Stink! I'm in the middle of an operation!" Judy pulled aside the tissue paper and lifted out the doctor doll.

At last! Judy held the doll in her lap and stroked her silky smooth hair. She made neat little bows in the ties of the doll's blue and white hospital gown. The doll was wearing a hospital bracelet.

"Her name is Hedda-Get-Betta," Judy read.

"Does she do anything?" asked Stink.

"It says here if you turn the knob on top of her head, she gets sick. Then you turn the knob again, and she gets betta. Get it?"

Judy turned the knob on the doll's head until a new face appeared. "She has measles!" said Stink.

"She talks when you hug her too." Judy hugged the doll.

"I have measles," said Hedda-Get-Betta.

Judy turned the knob until another face appeared. Then she hugged the doll again.

"I have chicken pox," said Hedda-Get-Betta.

"Cool," said Stink. "A sick doll. With three heads."

Judy turned the knob once more and hugged the doll. "All better," said Hedda.

"Can I make her get sick, then better?" asked Stink.

"No," said Judy. "I'm the doctor."

Judy opened her doctor kit. "At last I have someone to practice on," she said.

"You practice on me all the time," said Stink.

"Someone who doesn't complain."

"You'd complain too if you had to hold

up a lamp and get bandages all over you. Why can't I ever be Elizabeth Blackwell, First Woman Doctor?"

"For one thing, you're a boy."

"Can I put her arm in a sling?" asked Stink.

"No," said Judy. She held the ear scope up to Hedda's ear and turned on the light.

"Can I mix up some of this blood from your doctor kit?"

"Shh, I'm listening." She held the stethoscope on Hedda. Then she held it on Stink's chest. "Hmm."

"What?" said Stink. "What do you hear?"

"A heartbeat. This can mean only one thing."

"What?"

"You're alive!"

"Can I listen for a heartbeat?"

"Okay, okay. But first get me a glass of water to mix the blood in."

"You get it," said Stink.

"Don't touch anything until I get back," said Judy. "Don't even breathe."

As soon as Judy rounded the corner, Stink turned the knob on the doll's head. Measles. He turned the knob again. Chicken pox. Measles. Chicken pox. Measles. Chicken pox. Stink turned Hedda-Get-Betta's head back and forth, over and over, faster and faster.

"Uh-oh," said Stink.

"What?" Judy asked, returning with a sloshing glass of water.

"Her head is stuck," he said. Judy grabbed Hedda-Get-Betta away from Stink.

"I have chicken pox," Hedda said. Judy tried to turn the knob. The knob was stuck all right. It would not turn, no matter how hard Judy twisted and yanked and pulled. "I have chicken pox. I have chicken pox," Hedda said again and again.

"Her head is stuck on chicken pox!" Judy moaned.

"It's not my fault," said Stink.

"Is too! Now she'll never get better!" Judy took Hedda's pulse. She listened to Hedda's heart. She checked Hedda's forehead for a fever. "My first patient, and she's going to have chicken pox for the rest of her life!"

Judy took the doll to her mother. But Mom could not turn the knob, even with her best opening-pickle-jars twist. Judy took the doll to her father. But Dad could not get the doll's head to turn, even with his best opening-spaghetti-sauce turn.

"What are you going to do?" asked Dad.

"There's only one thing I can think of."

"Give her a shot?" asked Mom.

"No," said Judy. "Band-Aids!"

"Cool!" said Stink.

Stink and Judy put fancy Band-Aids on Hedda-Get-Betta's face, one for every chicken pock. Then they put Band-Aids all over her body. There were Endangered Species Band-Aids, Dinosaurs, Tattoos, Mermaids, and Race Cars. Even Glow-in-the-Dark Bloodshot-Eyeball Band-Aids.

"So she won't scratch," said Doctor Judy.

"I'm glad that emergency's over," Dad said.

Judy tried to turn the doll's head one last time. She did not yank or twist or pull. She very slowly, very carefully turned the knob. Hedda's head turned, and her smiling, no-chicken-pox face reappeared.

"I cured her!" Judy yelled. She hugged her doll. "All better," said Hedda-Get-Betta.

"Good as new," said Mom and Dad.

"I'm just glad she didn't have spotted fever," said Judy. "I never in a million years would have had enough Band-Aids for that!"

The T. P. Club

"I think it's going to rain for forty days and forty nights," said Stink.

Judy was hanging blankets from her top bunk to make a rain forest canopy over her bottom bunk. When that was done, she set Jaws on the top bunk for a jungly effect. Who needed a two-toed sloth? She climbed in and spread out her Me collage. Mouse climbed in after her. "Don't get hair on my collage," Judy warned her.

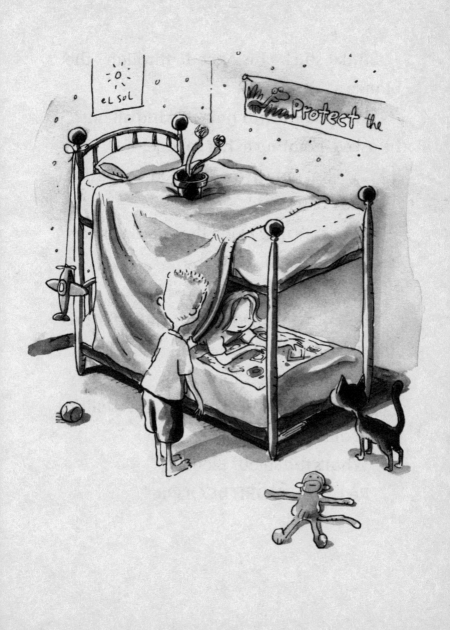

Stink stuck his head through the blankets.

"Who's that with hair sticking all out?" he asked, pointing to her collage.

"That's me in a bad mood on the first day of school."

"Where's me? Don't they need to know about brothers?"

"You mean *bothers?*" asked Judy.

She pointed to some dirt glued in the lower left-hand corner.

"I'm dirt?" asked Stink.

Judy cracked up. "That's for selling moon dust," said Judy.

"What's that blob? Blood?"

"Red. MY FAVORITE COLOR."

"Are those Spider Web Band-Aids?" Stink asked. "Where'd you get glitter glue? Can I come in there and glitter glue my bat wings?"

Her little brother, the bat freak, was becoming a regular Frank Pearl.

"There's no room, Stink. This is serious. I only have about two more weeks to finish."

Judy cut out a picture of Hedda from the ad in her *Luna Girls* magazine and pasted it in the doctor corner, right next to her drawing of Elizabeth Blackwell copied from an encyclopedia.

She checked Mr. Todd's list of collage ideas.

CLUBS. I don't belong to any clubs,

thought Judy. She'd have to skip that one.

HOBBIES. Collecting things was her favorite hobby. But she couldn't paste a scab or a Barbie head to the collage. She taped on the pizza table from her newest collection—the one Mr. Todd had given her.

THE WORST THING THAT EVER HAPPENED. She couldn't think of anything. Maybe the worst thing that ever happened to her hadn't happened yet.

THE FUNNIEST THING THAT EVER HAPPENED. When I knocked real spooky on the wall of Stink's room one night and scared him, she thought. But how could she put that on a collage?

Judy puzzled over her Me collage until the rain finally stopped. She called Rocky.

"Meet me at the manhole in five," she told him.

Rocky wore his boa constrictor shirt. Judy wore her boa constrictor shirt. "Same-same!" said Judy and Rocky, slapping hands together twice in a high-five, the way they always had when they did something exactly alike.

Judy and Rocky stood on the manhole. "What do you think is under the street?" asked Rocky.

"Oodles and oodles of worms," said Judy.

"Let's collect some in the street and throw them down there," said Rocky.

"Too oogley," said Judy.

"We could look for rainbows in puddles," Rocky suggested.

"Too hard!" said Judy.

"Listen," said Rocky. "I hear toads. We could catch toads!"

Rocky ran back home to get a bucket. When he came back, they cornered a toad and popped the bucket on top of it.

"Gotcha!" Judy held it in her hand. "It feels soft and bumpy. It's kind of cool, but not slimy."

All of a sudden, Judy felt something warm and wet in her hand. "Yuck!" she cried. "That toad peed on me." She tossed the toad back into the bucket.

"It's probably just wet from the rain," Rocky said.

"Oh, yeah? Then you pick it up." Rocky picked up the toad. He held it in his hand. It

felt soft and bumpy and cool-but-not-slimy all at once.

Just then Rocky felt something warm and wet in his hand. "Yuck," Rocky cried. "Now that toad peed on me." He tossed the toad back into the bucket.

"See what I mean?" said Judy. "I can't believe it happened to both of us the same!"

"Same-same!" said Rocky, and they double-high-fived. "Now it's like we're members of the same club. A secret club that only the two of us know about."

"And now we have a club to put on our Me collages," said Judy.

"What should we call it?" asked Rocky.

"The Toad Pee Club!"

"Rare!" said Rocky. "We could put T. P.

Club on our collages. People will think it stands for the Toilet Paper Club."

"Perfect," Judy said.

"Hey, what are you two doing?" asked Stink, running down the sidewalk in too-big boots.

"Nothing," said Judy, wiping her hands down the sides of her pants.

"Yes, you are," said Stink. "I can tell by your caterpillar eyebrow."

"What caterpillar eyebrow?"

"Your eyebrows make a fuzzy caterpillar when you don't want to tell me something." Judy Moody never knew she had caterpillar eyebrows before.

"Yeah, a stinging caterpillar," said Judy.

"We're starting a club," said Rocky.

"A secret club," Judy said quickly.

"I like secrets," said Stink. "I want to be in the club."

"You can't just be in the club," said Judy. "Something has to happen to you."

"I want the thing to happen to me too."

"No, you don't," said Judy.

"It's yucky," Rocky said.

"What?" asked Stink.

"Never mind," said Judy.

"You have to pick up that toad," Rocky told Stink.

"This is a trick, isn't it?" asked Stink. "To get me to pick up a slimy, bumpy old toad."

"That's right," said Judy.

Stink picked up the toad anyway. "Hey, it feels . . . interesting. Like a pickle. I never

picked up a toad before," said Stink. "Now
can I be in the club?"

"No," said Judy.

"I can't believe it's not slimy," said Stink.

"Just wait," said Rocky.

"I'm not going to get warts or anything, am I?"

"Do you feel anything?" asked Rocky.

"No," said Stink.

"Oh, well," said Judy. "Put the toad back. There. See? You can't be in the club."

Stink started to cry. "But I picked up the toad, and I want to be in the club."

"Don't cry," said Judy. "Trust me, Stink, you don't want to be in this club."

Just then Stink's eyes opened very wide. There was something warm and wet on his hand. Judy Moody and Rocky fell down laughing.

"Am I in the club yet?" asked Stink.

"Yes! Yes! Yes!" said Judy and Rocky. "The Toad Pee Club!"

"Yippee!" cried Stink. "I'm in the Toad Pee Club!"

The Worst Thing Ever

D-day. Doomsday. Dumbday. Saturday. The day of Frank Eats-Paste Pearl's birthday party. I'd rather eat ten jars of paste myself than go to that party, Judy thought.

For three whole weeks she had kept the hand-delivered-by-Frank-Pearl birthday invitation hidden inside the bottom of her Tip-It game, where Mom and Dad (who hated Tip-It) would NEVER find it.

Then today, the very day of the party, it happened. Dad found out.

She, Judy Moody, just had to ask Dad to take her to Fur & Fangs for some toad food. She just happened to be looking at a tadpole kit with real live frog eggs—*Watch tadpoles turn into frogs! See tails shrink, feet grow, legs form!*—hoping to talk Dad into buying it for her when another kit just like it bumped into her. Holding the kit was Frank's mom.

"Judy!" Frank's mom said. "Isn't that funny? It looks like we had the same idea for Frank's present! I thought he'd love watching a tadpole turn into a frog. I was about to buy him the same kit!"

"Um, I wasn't . . . I mean, you were?"

"Frank's really looking forward to seeing you at his party."

"Party?" Dad's ears perked up. "Whose party?"

"Frank's!" said his mom. "I'm Mrs. Pearl, Frank's mom."

"Nice to meet you," said Dad.

"Very nice to meet *you*," said Mrs. Pearl. "And Judy, I'll see you this afternoon. Bye for now."

Mrs. Pearl put the tadpole kit she was holding back on the shelf.

"Frank LOVES reptiles," she said.

Amphibians, thought Judy.

"Judy, why didn't you just say you needed to come here to get your friend a birthday present? Did I know you had a party to go to today?" Dad asked.

"No."

In the car, Judy tried to convince her Dad that there would be kids at the party making rude body noises and calling each other animal-breath names.

"You'll have fun."

"You know, Frank Pearl eats paste," said Judy.

"Look. You've already got the tadpole kit," Dad said.

"I was kind of sort of hoping I could keep it."

"But Mrs. Pearl put hers back when she saw yours. At least take it over, Judy."

"Do I have to wrap it?" asked Judy.

From the look on his face, she knew the answer.

Judy Moody wrapped the too-good-for-a-paste-eater present in boring newspaper  (not the comics). Even though the party started at two o'clock, she told Mom and Dad that the party didn't start until four o'clock, so she would only have to go for the last disgusting minutes.

The whole family rode in the car to Frank Pearl's house. Even Toady went along, carried by Stink in a yogurt container. Judy held Frank's lumpy present and fell into a bad-mood back-seat slump. Why did Rocky have to go to his grandma's TODAY of all days?

"She's crying!" Stink reported to the front seat.

"Am not!" she said back with her best troll eyes ever.

"Wait here," Judy told her family when they got to Frank's house.

"Go ahead. Have fun," Dad said. "We'll be back for you in half an hour. Forty minutes tops."

"We're only going to the supermarket," said Mom. But they might as well have been going to New Zealand.

Mrs. Pearl answered the door. "Judy! We thought you'd changed your mind. C'mon out back."

"Fra-ank. Judy's here, honey," Mrs. Pearl called out to the backyard.

Judy looked around the yard. All she could see were boys. Boys hurling icing insects at each other and boys mixing chocolate cake with ketchup and boys conducting an experiment with Kool-Aid and a grasshopper.

"Where are the other kids?" asked Judy.

"Everybody's here, honey. Frank's little sister, Maggie, went off to a friend's. I think you know all the boys from school. And there's Adrian and Sandy from next door."

Sandy was a boy. So was Adrian. That

Frank Pearl had tricked her—the girls next door were boys! She, Judy Moody, was definitely the one and only girl. Alone. At Frank Pearl's all-boy-except-her birthday party!

Judy wanted to climb right up Frank Pearl's tire-swing rope and howl like a rain forest monkey. Instead she asked, "Do you have a bathroom?"

Judy decided to stay in the Pearls' bathroom forever. Or at least until her parents came back from New Zealand. Frank Pearl's all-boy party had to be THE WORST THING THAT EVER HAPPENED to her.

Judy looked for something to do. Uncapping an eyebrow pencil, she drew some sharp new teeth on her faded first-day-of-school shark T-shirt. Rare.

Knock knock.

"Ju-dy? Are you in there?" Judy turned on the water in a hurry so Mrs. Pearl would think she was washing her hands.

"Just a minute!" she called. Water sprayed her all over, soaking her shirt. The sharp new shark teeth blurred and ran.

Judy opened the door. Mrs. Pearl said, "Frank was about to open your present, but we couldn't find you."

Back outside, Brad pointed at Judy's wet shirt. "You guys! It's a shark! With black blood dripping from its mouth!"

"Cool!" "Wow!" "How'd you do that?"

"Talent," said Judy. "And water."

"Water fight!" Brad took a glass of water and threw it on Adam. Mitchell threw one at Dylan. Frank poured one right over his own head and grinned.

Mrs. Pearl whistled, which put a stop to the water battle. "Dylan! Brad! Your parents are here. Don't forget your party favors." Mrs. Pearl gave a baby Slinky to each kid as he went out the door. By the time she got to Judy, there were no more baby Slinkies left.

"I must have counted wrong," said Mrs. Pearl.

"Or Brad took two," said Frank.

"Here, Judy. I was going to buy these for party favors, but I couldn't find enough." Mrs. Pearl handed her a miniature rock-and-gem collection in a plastic see-through box! Tiny amethyst and jade stones. Even a crackly amber one.

"Thank you, Mrs. Pearl!" Judy said, and she meant it. "I love collecting stones and things. Once my brother thought he found a real moon rock!"

"Frank's a collector too," said Mrs. Pearl. "All the boys are gone, Frank. Why don't you take Judy up to your room and show her while she waits for her parents?"

"C'mon. Last one up's a rotten banana!" said Frank.

He probably collects paste jars, Judy thought. He probably eats it for a midnight snack.

Frank Pearl's shelves were lined with coffee cans and baby food jars. Each one was filled with marbles, rubber bugs, erasers, something. Judy couldn't help

asking, "Do you have any baseball erasers?"

"I have ten!" said Frank. "I got them FREE when a real Oriole came to the library."

"Really? Me too!" Judy smiled. She almost said "Same-same," then caught herself just in time.

"I'm taping one to my Me collage, beside my favorite bug, a click beetle, for HOBBIES—you know, collecting things."

"That's my hobby too," Judy told him.

He also had two pencil sharpeners—a Liberty Bell and a brain—and a teeny-tiny flip-book from Vic's. Frank Pearl showed her his buffalo nickel, which he kept in a double-locked piggy bank. "It's not really a collection yet because there's only one."

"That's okay," said Judy.

Frank also had a killer comic-book collection, with really old ones like the Green Hornet, Richie Rich, and Captain Marvel. To top it off, he even had a miniature soap collection, with fancy hotel names on the wrappers.

Judy forgot all about wanting to leave. "What's that?" she asked.

"A pitcher plant. It catches insects. They think it's a flower, so they land on it. Then they fall down this tube, and the plant eats them."

"Rare!" said Judy. "I have a Venus flytrap named Jaws."

"I know," said Frank. "That was funny when you brought it to school, how it ate that hamburger and stunk up your back-pack and everything."

"Fra-ank! Ju-dy! The Moodys are here."

"I guess I gotta go," Judy told Frank.

"Well, thanks for the tadpole kit," Frank said, twisting a leg of the rubber click beetle from his collection.

"Hey, do you really eat paste?" asked Judy.

"I tasted it one time. For a dare."

"Rare!" Judy said.

Definitely the Worst Thing Ever

Judy's day was off to a grouchy start. This was the day that Stink, her once smelly, sold-dirt-for-moon-dust brother was going with his class to Washington, D.C., to see the president's house!

She found out Mom and Dad were going too, as chaperones.

Yours Truly had to stay home and finish her Me collage. She, Judy Moody, still had several bald spots to fill.

"I think my brain has a leak," Judy told her family. "I can't think of one more interesting thing to put on my collage."

Judy sank down on the family-room couch like a balloon that had lost three days' air. "Interesting things could happen to me better in Washington, D.C.," said Judy.

"You know it's just for the second-grade classes, honey," said Mom.

"ROAR!" was all she said.

"We might be home late," Dad told her. "You can go to Rocky's after school. You two can finish up your projects together."

"You'll have fun," said Mom. "And aren't you going to an assembly today for Brush Your Teeth Week?"

How could she forget? One more reason to be grouchy. Stink got to rub elbows with the president while she, Judy Moody, would be shaking the hands of Mr. Tooth and Mrs. Floss.

Stink waddled into the family room wrapped in a red and white striped table-cloth, looking like he just got hit by a flying picnic.

"What's that?" asked Judy.

"It's a costume, for my YOU ARE THE FLAG project. I'm the flag."

"Stink, you're not supposed to *be* the flag. You're supposed to tell what the flag means to you."

"To me it means I *am* the flag."

"What's on your head?"

"A hat. See, each star is a state, like on the flag. There's one for all forty-eight states."

"Guess what. There are fifty states, Stink."

"Nuh-uh. I counted. I crossed them off on my map."

"Count again," Judy said. "You probably forgot Hawaii and Alaska."

"Do you think the president will notice?" asked Stink.

"Stink, the president just about made the states. He'll notice."

"Okay, okay. I'll stick two more on."

"Every other second-grader writes a flag poem or draws a picture for YOU ARE THE FLAG. *My* brother's a human flag."

"What's wrong with that?"

"You look like a star-spangled mummy and walk like a banana. That's what."

"I get to see a room where everything is made of real gold. Even the curtains and bedspreads. Heather Strong says the lamps are made of diamonds."

"Heather Strong lies," said Judy.

It was no use. She would have to change her Me collage. Frank's birthday party was no longer THE WORST THING EVER. Frank Pearl ate paste for a dare! And he gave her a baby food jar with six ants and a fly for Jaws.

Not meeting the president of her own United fifty States was absolutely and positively THE WORST THING THAT EVER

HAPPENED. Her whole family, including her brother, the human flag, was going to Washington, D.C., while she, Judy Moody, would be listening to a talking tooth.

The Funniest Thing Ever

It was pouring outside. Judy's dad would not let her leave for school without an umbrella, and the only one she could find was her first-grade yellow ducky one. She wouldn't open a baby umbrella, so she got soaked clear through. The sun is probably shining over the president's house this second, thought Judy. She felt like a bike left out in the rain.

"Frank wants to come over after school too," Rocky told her on the bus. "And I have a brand new ten-dollar bill from Nay-Nay. We can go to Vic's after school and buy something really rare."

"Do they have any real gold at Vic's?" was all she said.

In Spelling, Judy wrote WEASELS when Mr. Todd had really said MEASLES. In Science, when Jessica Finch threw Judy the ball of yarn for their giant spider web, she dropped it. It rolled out the door just when Ms. Tuxedo, the principal, walked past in high heels. And at the Brush Your Teeth Week assembly, Mr. Tooth picked Judy to be a cavity. On stage. In front of the whole school.

She could not get her mind off Stink at the president's house, where *she* wasn't. Seeing all that real gold. Would he get to shake the president's hand? Meet the president's daughter? Sit in a gold chair?

"Are flags allowed to talk?" she asked Frank.

"Only if they're talking flags!"

That did it. There would be no living with Stink once he had been to the president's.

On the bus ride home, Rocky squirted Frank with his magic nickel. Frank snorted, wiping the drips on his sleeve. Judy pretended it was funny. Really she was thinking, Stink could be petting the president's puppy, right now, this very instant. When

Rocky said, "I can't wait to go to Vic's," Judy grunted.

The three of them half-ran through leftover puddles all the way to Vic's. Rocky didn't even stop to cross through China and Japan the right way. "What's the big hurry?" she asked.

"I need something," said Rocky, "but there's only one left, and I want to make sure I get it!" he said. When they got to Vic's, Rocky went straight to the counter.

"Over here," Rocky told them. "There's still one left!"

Judy stood on tiptoes to look in a box on top of the counter. Lying in the bottom was . . . a hand. A person's hand! Judy almost screamed. Frank almost screamed too. Then they realized it was made out of rubber.

"What do you think?" asked Rocky.

"Rare," said Judy.

"Ace," said Frank. "It looks so real. Fingernails and everything!"

Rocky bought the hand and three fireballs.

"What are you going to do with your hand?" Frank asked.

"I don't know," said Rocky. "I just like it."

When they got to Rocky's house, Judy tried to work on her Me collage. But she was not in a FUNNIEST THING EVER mood. All the funny stuff that had ever happened to her seemed to have gotten up and left. Marched right out of her brain like a line of ants from a picnic.

Rocky showed Judy and Frank his finished collage. "Here's Thomas Jefferson in the window of my house for WHERE I LIVE. I cut him out of play money."

"That's good!" said Frank. "For Jefferson Street."

"The piece of cloth is part of my sling from when I broke my arm, THE WORST THING EVER."

"And here's a toilet paper roll for the T. P. Club, a secret club I'm in," Rocky said, glancing at Judy.

"What kind of club has toilet paper?" asked Frank.

"If I tell you, it won't be a secret,"

"Who's this?" Frank asked Rocky, pointing to a lizard.

"Houdini, MY FAVORITE PET."

"And who's that guy, walking through a brick wall?" Frank asked.

"That's my favorite part. My mom made a copy of a picture of the real Harry Houdini from a library book."

Judy touched a clump of garlic. "Are you trying to scare away vampires or something?"

"That's from one time when I ate a whole thing of garlic by mistake. THE FUNNIEST THING EVER was that I stunk like a skunk for a week!"

"Like Jaws when it ate that hamburger!" said Frank.

"Like Stink when he takes his smelly shoes off," said Judy.

"Is this you?" Frank asked.

"That's me in my magician hat, making a fishbowl disappear."

"Too bad you can't make Stink disappear," said Judy.

"Too bad I'm done," said Rocky. "It would have been really funny to put the rubber hand on my collage."

That's when it happened. An idea. The funniest of all funnies. It orbited Judy's head and landed like a spaceship, the way good ideas do.

"Rocky! You're a genius! Let's go to my

house," Judy said. "And bring the hand."

"You're *not* a genius," said Rocky. "Nobody's home at your house. We could get into all kinds of trouble."

"Exactly!" said Judy. "C'mon. There's a key hidden in the gutter pipe."

"Did you forget something?" asked Frank.

"Yes," Judy said. "I forgot to play a trick on Stink!"

Once inside, Judy raced around her house, looking for the perfect spot to leave the hand, a place where Stink would be sure to find it right away. The couch? Toady's aquarium? The refrigerator? Under his pillow?

The bathroom!

Where?

Here?

How about here?

Hmm...

Or here?

Maybe here?

I've got it!

Perfect!

In the downstairs bathroom, Judy lifted up the toilet seat, just a crack, and perched the hand there, its fingernails hanging over the edge. "It looks real," said Rocky.

"This will scare the president right out of him," said Judy. "For sure."

Back at Rocky's, Judy, Frank, and Rocky knelt on Rocky's bed, looking out the window. Every time a car zoomed by on Jefferson Street, they yelled, "It's them!" Finally Judy saw a blue van, for real. "Run!" she yelled. "They're pulling into the driveway!"

Stink was so excited telling Judy, Rocky, and Frank all about the president's house that Hawaii and Alaska fell off his hat.

Why doesn't he go to the bathroom? thought Judy.

"There's a movie theater—I swear! Inside the president's house. And a room with a secret door. No lie. Even a clock that tells you when it's time to take a bath," said Stink.

"Rare!" said Judy. "You need one of those."

Go into the bathroom, Stink, she wished silently. As if he had heard, Stink stopped his story. Balancing his hat on his head, he walked into the bathroom and shut the door behind him. The lock clicked.

Mom and Dad asked Judy about the Mr. Tooth assembly, but her ears were tuned to the bathroom. "AAAAAHHHHH!" screamed Stink. He burst out of the bathroom, hat crashing to the floor, stars flying.

"Hey! Dad! Mom! There's somebody in the toilet!"

Judy Moody, Rocky, and Frank Pearl fell on the floor laughing.

The Me Collage

Stink watched Judy finish her collage after school the next day. "Almost done," said Judy. "It's due tomorrow."

Stink pointed. "You still have a bald spot right there next to the picture of Jaws."

Judy carefully taped a doll hand from her collection over the empty space. "Not anymore," she said.

"That hand? Is it for the trick you played on me?" asked Stink.

"Yes. It's THE FUNNIEST THING EVER," said Judy, with a grin.

"You mean you're going to tell your whole class I thought there was somebody in our toilet?"

"Stink, I'm making you famous."

"Couldn't you change my name or something?" asked Stink.

"Or something," said Judy.

When Judy got up the next morning, it was pouring rain again. Something told her to get ready for a bad-mood Friday.

"Let's put your Me collage in a garbage bag so it won't get wet," Dad suggested when she brought it downstairs.

"Dad, I'm not carrying my Me collage in a garbage bag."

"Why not?"

"Did Van Gogh put his *Starry Night* in a garbage bag?"

"She's got a point there," said Mom.

"Garbage bags probably hadn't been invented yet," said Dad. "If Van Gogh had garbage bags, believe me, he would have been smart enough to use them."

"Honey, why don't you take the bus, and Dad'll bring your collage to school after he takes Stink to the dentist?" Mom said. "Stink's taking Toady to school today, so Dad has to drop him off anyway."

"I want to take my collage to school myself. That way I can be sure nothing will happen to it."

"What could happen to it?" asked Mom.

"There could be a tornado," said Stink, "and the wind could make you drop it, and it could get run over by a bus."

"Hardee, har, har," said Judy.

"You do have a lot of other stuff to carry," said her dad. Judy had her lunch, her dad's lab coat so she could dress like a doctor for her talk, Hedda-Get-Betta, her doctor kit, and plenty of Band-Aids.

"Okay," she said, "but don't squish anything and don't get it wet and it has to be there by eleven o'clock and don't let Stink do *anything*." She gave her brother her best troll-eyes stare.

"We'll be careful," said Dad.

Judy rode the bus with Rocky, who

practiced his Squirting Nickel magic trick on her for the one-hundredth time.

"Okay! It works!" Judy told him, wiping drips from her face. Rocky cracked up.

All morning, Judy imagined things happening to her collage. What if it fell into a puddle when her father opened the car door? What if Toady got out of Stink's pocket and peed on the collage? What if a tornado came, like Stink said . . .

Eleven o'clock came, and her collage still was not there. No sign of Stink. Or Dad.

Judy could hardly listen to the other kids showing their Me collages. She kept her eyes glued to the door of 3T.

"Judy, would you like to go next?" asked Mr. Todd, startling her.

"I'd like to go last," said Judy.

"Frank?"

"I'd like to go last too," said Frank. "After Judy."

Judy looked at Frank's desk. "Where's your Me collage?" she asked him.

"I didn't bring it. I mean, I'm not finished. I still don't have a CLUB," Frank whispered. "Where's yours?"

"My brother's supposed to bring it," said Judy. She glanced at the door again. There he was! Stink motioned for her to come out in the hall.

Stink looked sick. "What's wrong?" Judy asked.

"If I tell you," said Stink, "you'll be in the worst mood ever."

"Where is it?" asked Judy. "Did you drop my collage in a puddle? Did Toady pee on it?"

"No," said Stink. "Not that."

"Where is it?" she asked again.

"Dad's in the boys' room. Drying it off."

Judy ran down to the boys' room, pushed the door open, and went right in. Crumpled paper towels were everywhere. "Dad!"

"Judy!"

"Is it ruined? Let me see!"

Dad held up her collage. Right smack dab in the center was a big purple stain the size of a pancake. Not a silver dollar one either. A giant, jaggedy triangle — a grape-colored lake floating in the middle of her collage!

"What happened?" Judy yelled.

"I was drinking Jungle Juice from a box," said Stink, standing behind her in the doorway, "and trying this thing with my straw. . . . I'm sorry."

"Stink! You wrecked it. Dad! How could you let him drink Jungle Juice in the car?"

"Look, it's not that bad," he said. "It almost looks like it's supposed to be there. I'll speak with Mr. Todd. Maybe he'll let you have the weekend and we can fix it. Cover it up somehow."

"Maybe we can erase it," said Stink. "With a giant eraser."

"Let me see." Judy held up the collage, looking it over. Even with the purple stain, she could still see the rain forest with Doctor

Judy Moody in the very middle. And none of the Band-Aids had come off.

"Never mind," said Judy.

"Never mind?" asked Dad.

"It's okay," she said. "At least it didn't get run over by a bus in a tornado."

"It's okay?" asked Stink. "You mean you're not going to put a rubber foot in my bed or anything?"

"No," said Judy. She grinned at her brother. "But that is a good idea."

"Look, honey. I know you worked forever on this. We'll make it up to you somehow."

"I know what to do. Stink, let me have your black marker." They all went out into the hall, and Stink dug a marker out of his

backpack. Judy set the collage on the floor and drew a black outline around the big purple triangle.

"Are you cuckoo?" asked Stink. "That's just going to make it stand out more."

"That's what I want," said Judy. "Then it'll look like it was supposed to be there all the time."

"I'm proud of you, Judy," said Dad. "The

way you took an accident like this and turned it into something good."

"What's it supposed to be?" Stink asked.

"Virginia," she said. "The state of Pocahontas and Thomas Jefferson. The place WHERE I LIVE."

Band-Aids and Ice Cream

When Judy got back to class, she put on her doctor coat, walked to the front of the room, and held her Me collage high. She stood tall, as if her brother had not nearly ruined her masterpiece with Jungle Juice. She tried to look like a person who would grow up to be a doctor and make the world a better place. A person who could turn a bad mood right around.

Judy told about herself and her family, including the time Stink sold moon dust, which explained why her brother was a piece of dirt. She traced the outline of Virginia with her finger to show where she lived. She talked about Rocky, her best friend, and Frank, her new friend. She pointed to a paste jar lid taped to a corner and told the class that Frank ate paste for a dare once.

"Is that Jaws?" asked Brad. "The thing that eats bugs?"

"Yes," said Judy. "Even though I have a cat, Jaws is MY FAVORITE PET. When I grow up and become a doctor, I want to move to the rain forest and search for medicines in rare plants that could cure ucky diseases."

Judy pointed out the pizza table from Mr. Todd and other stuff she collected for HOBBIES. She told the class that she was a member of the T. P. Club, but that she couldn't tell them what T. P. stood for.

"This is a picture my parents took of Stink, standing outside the White House in his flag costume." And she explained why it was THE WORST THING THAT EVER HAPPENED to her. Everybody's favorite part of her collage was when she showed the doll hand, coming out of a magazine toilet. So Judy told them about how the worst thing ever turned into THE FUNNIEST THING EVER.

"Any questions?" she asked the class.

"Who's the old lady?" asked Frank.

Judy explained about Elizabeth Black-well, First Woman Doctor, and then gave a demonstration of her doctor skills. She put Rocky's arm in a sling and wrapped bandages around Frank's knee. She pulled out her pretend blood, and used Hedda-Get-Betta to show how to apply Band-Aids.

"That's it. Me. Judy Moody."

"Great job, Judy," said Mr. Todd. "Class, any comments?"

"I like how you painted Virginia in the middle of your collage to show where you live," said Jessica Finch, "instead of just using a picture of your house."

"Those Tattoo Band-Aids are the coolest," said Dylan. "I have a blister. Can I have one?"

"I have a hangnail!"

"I have a paper cut!"

"I have a mosquito bite!"

Before Judy knew it, everybody in the whole class was wearing Tattoo Band-Aids.

"Judy Moody, you're a mover and a shaker," said Mr. Todd.

"I am?" asked Judy. "What's that mean?"

Mr. Todd laughed. "Let's just say it means you have imagination."

What had almost become a bad-mood Friday had turned into one very fine day.

And it wasn't over yet.

When she walked out to get the bus that afternoon, Mom and Dad were waiting to take Judy and Stink for ice cream at Screamin' Mimi's.

"I'm getting that blue ice cream, Rain Forest Mist. Like you guys always do!" Stink jumped up and down, holding his pocket with the toad.

"Did your teacher like Toady?" Judy asked.

"Yes, but she was almost in the Toad Pee Club," said Stink. Judy cracked up.

"Mom, Dad, can I ask Rocky and Frank to come too?"

"That's a great idea," Mom said.

Outside Screamin' Mimi's, Judy licked

her Rain Forest Mist scoop on top of Chocolate Mud, her favorite. She was in her best Judy Moody mood ever.

Stink took Toady out of his pocket and set him on the picnic table. Toady hopped toward a blue drip from Rocky's ice cream cone.

"Toady likes Rain Forest Mist!" said Rocky.

"Hey, Frank," Judy asked, "when are you going to finish your Me collage?"

"Mr. Todd said I could bring it on Monday."

"You're not done yet?" asked Rocky.

"I *still* don't have anything for CLUBS. The dictionary says a club is three or more people."

Judy looked at Rocky. Rocky looked at Stink. Stink looked at Judy. All three of them looked at Frank.

"If you pick up Toady right now, you can be in a club," said Judy.

"Really?" asked Frank.

"Really and truly," said Judy and Rocky at the same time.

Frank crinkled his nose. "I don't get it."

Rocky laughed. "You will."

Frank scooped up Toady with one hand.

"Use both hands," said Judy.

"Like this," said Rocky, cupping his hands.

"Just hold him a minute," said Stink.

"I still don't get it," said Frank.

"Oh, you'll *get* it," said Judy, Rocky, and Stink.

A second later, Frank felt something warm and wet in his hand. He crossed his eyes, and they all fell down laughing.